MY BABY'S GONE

MY BABY'S GONE

MARLIN CRONE

DEDICATION

This book is dedicated to my family.

Paperback ISBN 978-1-960007-54-4
eBook ISBN 978-1-960007-55-1

Published by

Orison Publishers, Inc.

PO Box 188
Grantham, PA 17027
www.OrisonPublishers.com

Unless otherwise indicated, all Scripture quotations are taken from the King James Version of the Bible. Public domain.

INTRODUCTION

I'm writing this book because I don't want you to be left behind. I grew up on a farm, and one summer day when I was young, my dad, my brother and I were irrigating the fields. They told me to go down to the creek and put more pressure on the pump so the water would come out better. They said they would be there when I came up. However, when I came up from the creek, I couldn't find them anywhere. I had no idea where they were. I thought the Lord had come and I was left behind. I don't know if you have ever had such a horrible feeling in the pit of your stomach as I had that day. I never forgot it. The rapture hadn't happened (but it will). I believe the things I have written about here will happen more than the sun will come up in the morning. I hope you will be ready after reading that this event will happen. I want to see you all over there.

MY BABY'S GONE!

Well, I'd better get up—it's almost 7:00 am. *Why isn't my baby up yet? She usually is squirming around by this time.* The sun is just coming up. It's going to be a beautiful day! A few minutes later, I peek into her crib. My baby's gone! *Where is she? Who took her?* Her little nightclothes are lying in her crib along with her diaper. Wait, there are her little diamond earrings. *Why would someone take my baby and take off all her clothes?* I didn't hear a thing! Where could she be? I reach down and touch her little blanket. It's cold, like she has been missing for a while. She must have been gone for several hours. *Am I nuts? What could have happened?* I rush to pick up the phone to call 911, and all I get is a robotic voice telling me that the phone lines are busy. *What is going on? This is crazy!* I turn on the television, and the whole world seems to be in a state of shock. People are missing everywhere.

The morning news reporters are looking shocked as many of their colleagues are missing, just like my baby. They don't understand what happened through the night either! Suddenly, the broadcast is interrupted with a headline news alert. "We interrupt to bring this special report. People seem to be missing all around the world. Many planes have fallen from the sky; we assume the pilots vanished. Automobiles have crashed. Cars everywhere are damaged with no drivers in sight." The local reporters return to say there is a pile of at least thirty cars on the interstate. Some of the vehicles have people in them and some do not! There also are tractor trailers that went down over the embankment. *This is awful! What is going on?*

I wonder if Mom and Dad are home? It's Friday, and usually Mom is off that day while Dad goes to work. I try to call, but Mom is not answering the phone. It just rings and rings. It doesn't even go to voicemail. *Well, I'll just go to their house. It's only about two miles away.* I wonder if "it" really did happen! *I'm left behind!* I never went to church very much. I never had much interest in that religious stuff.

What am I going to do? Mom always tried to talk to me about spiritual things, but I just let it go in one ear and out the other. She used to mention something about the rapture. I never really believed it would happen. Now, I think, it really happened. *What am I going to do? I miss my baby!*

I jump in the car and drive over to my parents' house to see if Mom is home. I park the car and run up to the porch. Opening the door, I notice that the house is quiet. "Mom! Mom, are you home?" I yell. There's no answer. Panicking, I run from room to room. In my parents' bedroom, the bedspread is a little messed up, but no one is there. I slowly pull back the bedspread and blanket. Mom's antique watch and the fillings from her teeth are lying on the pillow. *Oh no, what's that?* Lower down, Mom's "kneecap" from her knee replacement surgery years ago is lying on the bed.

Nausea rolls in my stomach. I feel so sick! Mom and Dad's nightclothes lay flat under the blankets. On his side of the bed, Dad's dentures are on his pillow and his hip replacement is tucked in his pajamas. How could this be? *I think I am going to throw up!*

The Bible says that we are naked when we come into the world and we are naked when go out![1] My mom and dad are gone. My baby's gone! I can't go anywhere. The roads are blocked with wrecked cars and trucks. The

---

1 Job 1:21.

telephone poles are down. The water hydrants are gushing out water. Some of the houses are on fire. Everything is a mess. *Wait, Mom put a testament in my glove box when I bought my car. I wonder if it's still there?* Going out to my car, I rummage through the glove compartment. *Okay, here it is. I found it!* Then I decide to try to ride around and see if I can find out what is going on.

As I drive slowly down the road, I see one green car that looks like it's smoking. I can hear the car running. *I wonder if anyone is inside.* Pulling over, I hop out and run to the car. Clothing is draped on the seat, a watch on top and a pair of boots at the foot pedal. The driver must have been a man. Nearby is a white car on its side. I look in it and I see an empty baby seat. All the clothing is still strapped in the seat. I feel sick.

I look down at my phone, and the news says people are missing worldwide. They say the disappearance happened in this country at 4:00 a.m. Eastern Standard Time. They say it happened in a split second. Millions of people have vanished. Some are saying that aliens from outer space came and took them hostage, but they're not sure. Everybody is in a state of shock, perplexed to what has happened.

Ring! Oh, Freddy is calling!

"Hey, did you hear that your uncle is getting his backhoe to go dig up the preacher at the cemetery?"

"No, is that right?" The preacher died a month ago. Many people in his congregation said he preached about the rapture. He said that "the dead in Christ shall rise first," and then those who "remain shall be caught up together" and "meet the Lord in the air" (1 Thessalonians 4:16–17). My uncle must be going to dig up his grave and see if his body is in the casket.

"He said that if the clothing is there in the casket with no body, then he will believe what the Bible says!" Freddy told me.

When I get to the cemetery, there are a lot of people waiting around to see if the preacher is in the casket. Using his backhoe, my uncle digs down and grabs the cement top. The casket fits inside of the cement so that the casket doesn't decay and the ground doesn't fall in. Putting the cement top aside, he uses the backhoe bucket to get ahold of the lid of the casket. Guess what? There is no preacher! But his clothes are there, along with his Bible that they put in when they buried him.

Now my uncle wants to dig up another grave—Jim's. He tells us why. "Jim never went to church except when he was a little boy. My friend invited Jim to church one time, and he said, 'Screw the church.' Jim later told my friend that he went to church as a little boy, and one of the deacons came to him after the service and told him, 'If you ever come to church again, I want to see shoes on your feet!' That's why Jim never came to church again."

My uncle gets his backhoe and digs down at Jim's grave. He gets the cement top off the casing and puts it aside. Then he reaches down and pulls the lid open. Jim is in the casket! When he was buried, they put a beer can in his hand. Uncle closes the lid, puts the cement top back on, and fills in the hole with the soil.

Now my uncle believes the Bible, but it's too late to go up with the saints. We're left behind. What's going to happen now?

AFTER THE RAPTURE

I believe that after the rapture happens, there will be seven years left, which are divided in half (three and a half years plus three and a half years). All of this confusion will take place all over the world. (Read Matthew 23.) World War I and World War II will be like child's play compared to what will happen.

Satan will then reveal himself in the form of a man. Or, I should say, Satan will influence through this man. This man is called the

Antichrist, the Beast, the lawless one, the deceiver and a lot of other names! As he comes to power, people will think he is wonderful. He can call fire from the sky, and they will think he has all the answers. He will be very intelligent, and I imagine that he will be very good-looking. He will try to rule the world. He will make everyone, great and small, receive a mark on the forehead or on the hand. (I think it will be a computer chip.) That mark contains all the information about you, like your Social Security number, banking account numbers, your name, your health records, etc. If you don't receive the mark, which refers to his name (666), then you will not be able to buy or sell anything. If you do receive the mark, though, you will be pledging your allegiance to this system and you will be doomed to hell for all eternity!

One time I was pulling up to the drive-thru at a fast food restaurant, and I thought how handy it would be to just stick your hand out and they could just scan your hand. You wouldn't have to hunt for your credit card, and nobody could take the card from you and steal your identity!

Only you would know your number. The people of the earth would think, *What a great idea!* But woe to them who take this mark.

Can you understand now why some people rejected the vaccine shot for Covid-19? Do you see how the government of the world wants to force you to take it?

They—the government—is at you to be subject to the system, a central system. All I can say to you is, do not take the mark. Suppose you don't take the mark of the Beast (666). What are you going to do? You can buy food that has been dried. Those companies say it is good for twenty-five years. You can live on some mountain or in the wilderness for seven years. Or you can surrender your life to be killed and give your own blood for your salvation. There will be a lot of people who do that. I don't think that kind of death will be pretty. I used to think those martyrs would go up a set of stairs and then be exposed to a bloody guillotine with dead people lying all around with their heads cut off and blood and gore all around. But now I think their deaths will happen with a short pocketknife like those terrorists showed on television a few years ago. Those Christians knelt and let the terrorists slice their heads off. Anyway, it will be worth it rather than burn in hell for all eternity.

If you don't believe that Jesus is coming again, you'd better believe what the Bible says after that.

Some people will say that aliens from outer space came and took those missing people hostage. Stop and think for a moment. How do you think someone could take people out of their beds, cars, trucks, planes, fields, stores and factories and take their earrings off, their fillings out of their teeth, their eyeglasses, kneecaps and hip replacements out or off their bodies?

How do you think they would take even the people who died 2,000 years ago, bring them up from the grave, and put a beautiful white robe on them in a matter of seconds?

The Bible says all of this will happen in a "twinkling of an eye."[2] Only God could do this! That is awesome!

It says in the Bible that the sea will give up the dead.[3] I'm reminded of a man who requested that, when he died, his ashes be spread out over the Atlantic Ocean. That man will be brought out of the ocean during the rapture or a thousand years later during the white throne judgement.

Remember, both the apostle Paul and Peter said Jesus will come as a thief in the night.[4] That's the rapture. But the Bible also says that He will come and "every eye" will see Him (Revelation 1:7)!

---

2   1 Corinthians 15:52.
3   Revelation 20:13.
4   1 Thessalonians 5:2; 2 Peter 3:10.

If you are reading this after the rapture, you didn't see Him, did you? He came as a thief in the night. Now when He comes to the earth again, Scripture says that "every eye" will see Him. Years ago, preachers of the gospel never could understand that. How can people on one side of the earth see on the other side? (The answer today: cell phones.)

Let's go back to the topic of the rapture. Now, I'm a farmer. On my land, around a certain area, there used to be a small graveyard of about ten or so people. They were buried on my farm. The fourth or fifth previous owner of my farm destroyed the graveyard so he could farm straight through. Today, when I drive my tractor out through the field where that graveyard used to lie, I think about those verses in the Bible where it says, "…and the dead in Christ shall rise first: then we which are alive and remain shall be caught up together with them in the clouds, to meet the Lord in the air…" (1 Thessalonians 4:16–17). I thought I might see a few people coming out of the ground on my farm with their white robes on. Maybe in a split second. I also thought of people all across the world mowing the graveyards who might also see a whole lot of white-robed people appear like a flash before their eyes.

But as the days of Noah were, so shall also the coming of the Son of man be. For as in the days that were before the flood they were eating and drinking, marrying and giving in marriage, until the day that Noe [Noah] entered into the ark, and knew not until the flood came, and took them all away; so shall also the coming of the Son of man be. Then shall two be in the field; the one shall be taken, and the other left. Two women shall be grinding at the mill; the one shall be taken, and the other left. Watch therefore: for ye know not what hour your Lord doth come. But know this, that if the goodman of the house had known in what watch the thief would come, he would have watched, and would not have suffered his house to be broken up. Therefore be ye also ready: for in such an hour as ye think not the Son of man cometh. (Matthew 24:37–44)

But I would not have you to be ignorant, brethren, concerning them which are asleep [referring to believers who have died], *that ye sorrow not, even as others which have no hope. For if we believe that Jesus died and rose again, even so them also which sleep in Jesus will God bring with him. … For the Lord himself shall descend from heaven with a shout, with the voice of the archangel, and with the trump of God: and the dead in Christ shall rise first: then we which are alive and remain shall be caught up together with them in the clouds to meet the Lord in the air: and so shall we ever be with the Lord. Wherefore comfort one another with these words.* (1 Thessalonians 4:13–14,16–18)

Let's go back to the people who have disappeared. What happened to them? Where did they go? How did they go up through space? Space is far, far away, and it's cold. What happened to those people whom they call saints, along with all the little babies and children up to the age of accountability? I believe that age is different for some than others. For example, my cousin was autistic, and she lived to be in her twenties. The doctors said that she had the mental capacity of a child three or four years old. I believe she went to heaven because she hadn't reached the age of accountability. By the way, all those little babies that were aborted (some sixty to eighty million in the United States alone) will all be in heaven. Do you remember that movie about the little boy who died and come back to life again? It was based on the book *Heaven Is for Real* by Todd Burpo. That little boy went to heaven and saw his sister, whom he knew nothing about. He told his mom and dad that he saw her and talked to her, to their amazement. His mother had had a miscarriage, and that unborn baby was in heaven.

Who are the people who are raptured? These are the people who have asked the Lord Jesus Christ to come into their lives and have asked Him to forgive them of their sins.

If you are a good person and give all your time and money to the poor and even give your "body to be burned" (1 Corinthians 13:3), you still will go to hell just like all the rest of the people. There is only *one* way you can get to heaven. There are *not* a lot of ways to get there, as some people would have you believe.

The people who are raptured (disappear) get a new body. Their bodies are transformed into supernatural bodies.

The Bible says that when Jesus rose from the dead, He saw a few people and told them not to touch Him because He hadn't gone to the Father in heaven yet. He went up and came back and then later met with the eleven disciples. He came in on them without going through the door. He told Thomas to put his hand in His side. Then Thomas believed.[5]

Like Jesus after the resurrection, we who are transformed have a supernatural body. We will have perfect teeth; our hearing will

---

5 John 20.

be 100 percent; we can taste, smell, talk, walk, run, feel, and touch. There is no wax in our ears, no snot in our nose, and no stink on our breath, even in the morning. Our armpits won't stink and we won't have to pass gas. I'm not sure if we will need to sleep. The Bible says of the Lord, "He never sleeps or slumbers" (Psalm 121:4).

We will be very, very intelligent. I think we who are raptured will be able to know what earthly people are thinking. Jesus did, and the Bible says that we shall be like Him.[6] I believe that all the saints who have supernatural bodies will look like they did when they were in their twenties or thirties. We also will be much better-looking. We also will be able to sing better than the best singers of today.

Everything that you can think of that you couldn't do in your natural body, you will be able to do 100 percent in your new body. If you want

---

6   1 John 3:2.

to go somewhere 2,000 miles away, just think it, and you will be there in a split second. You wouldn't get cold or hot; you wouldn't be able to get killed. You don't have to go to the bathroom. What happens to the food and drink that you put in your supernatural body while you are at the marriage supper of the Lamb with Jesus and all your friends who made it? What happens to the food in your new body? I don't know, but I do know there are no commodes in heaven!

THE SEVEN-YEAR TRIBULATION AND BEYOND

Let's consider the time we are living in now. Do you think about how our leaders want to control us? Have you thought about how Covid-19 might have been a way for them to do so?

Some people love to hold power over other people. Years ago, I hired about eight young kids to work on my farm. One day, I told them that I was leaving for about two hours, and I told Johnny that he was the boss. I told them what to do, and little Johnny stood straight, put his shoulders back, and said, "Come on, you guys." He changed in a moment from employee to boss. People are the same way; they love that "power."

Today there is a lot of discontent in the world. Satan is working hard so that when we Christians are taken out of this world, he (the devil) will have a lot more power to accomplish his destructive plans. People will rise up and fight each other much more than they do today. Brother will hate brother, and sister will hate sister. Read your Bible and follow through what it says if you are still alive after the rapture.

I have heard people say that if you can't live for the Lord now in this time of grace, which is now, it will be 100 times harder during the time of the tribulation.

All I can say is, get your life ready now. Repent and ask God to forgive you of your sin. Ask Jesus to come in to your heart and live like He is coming today or tonight.

Remember what I wrote earlier. If you want to be a Christian after the rapture, you can give your life's blood for your redemption. It will hurt just a little while rather than hurt in hell for all eternity.

The Bible says not to worry about those who can kill the body. Rather, it says to fear the one who has the power to kill the body and soul.[7]

I don't know a lot about the seven-year tribulation, but I do know that it will be hell on earth. Personally, I think it will be nuclear war, along with other types of wars.

The Bible says that during this tribulation, the flesh will fall off of bodies before they fall to the ground.[8] That sounds like nuclear to me

A lot of things will take place in the seven years after the rapture. In the first three-and-a-half

---

7 Matthew 10:28.
8 Zechariah 14 and 2 Peter 3.

years, the Antichrist will make a peace treaty with Israel, and they will rebuild the temple in Jerusalem. Israel has wanted to do this for a long time. But after three-and-a-half years, the Antichrist, the Beast, will break his promise and cut off the peace treaty. This is called the "abomination that maketh desolate" spoken of by Daniel the prophet standing in the Holy Place (Daniel 12:11). The next period of time, the last three-and-a-half years of the tribulation, is going to be bad, very bad.

God will send two witnesses to the earth. We believe it will be Enoch and Elijah, for they hadn't died when they lived on this earth thousands of years ago; instead, they were raptured.

According to Revelation 11, these two men will have the power to not allow it to rain. They have power over the water, to turn it into blood. They will send all kinds of plagues, as often as they wish (frogs, boils on people's bodies, hundred-pound balls of hail). Have you experienced a storm with hail as big as baseballs? The sky gets dark!

If anyone tries to kill these two witnesses, they will devour their would-be killers with fire out of their mouths, killing them. The Antichrist will eventually kill the two witnesses. Then it will be like Christmas all over the world. People will give presents to one another. The bodies of these two men will lie on the ground for three days. The news will televise their dead bodies lying on the street. Then, after three days, they will come alive again.

Great fear will fall upon the people who see them. I imagine that the television cameras and cell phones will be on these two witnesses, and people will see them all over the world. Then a voice from heaven will call them up, and the two will be raptured up.

As the last part of the tribulation comes to an end, there will be 200 million men going to battle at Armageddon. The Bible says that in the valley, the blood will flow up to a horse's bridle. That's three feet deep.[9]

The Bible says that if God doesn't shorten the days, all flesh will be gone except for His elect, which is the Jewish people.[10]

There are a whole lot of people who are left when the rapture takes place. These people will get killed by war, famine, diseases, and pestilence, and some people will give their lives for the sake of living a Christian life.

Even so, there will be people here on earth when Jesus returns. They will see Him appear in the sky with millions and millions of His people with Him. The Bible says they will weep and wail and shout for joy![11]

Those of us who were raptured are all coming back to earth after seven years in heaven.

---

9   Revelation 14 and 16.
10   Matthew 24:22.
11   Revelation 1:7.

He, the Christ, will set up His kingdom on this earth in Israel, and the capital will be Jerusalem.

The battle of Armageddon will be taking place. The Antichrist will try to wage war on Jesus and the saints when he sees us in the sky. But Jesus will speak, and the armies will die. Then He, Jesus, will throw the Antichrist (the Beast) and the false prophet in hell for ever and ever.

Jesus will next take the devil (Satan) and throw him into the bottomless pit for 1,000 years.

The people who are left on the earth, who have their fleshly bodies, will live on the earth. The Jewish people will then accept Jesus as their king.

They will populate the earth again. But what about the people who came back with Jesus, who have supernatural bodies? They are the ones who will rule and reign and keep order. The Bible says Jesus will rule with a rod of iron.[12]

---

12 Revelation 19:15.

Israel will be the capital of the world, and Jesus Himself will be King of kings and Lord of lords.

What will happen on the earth in the thousand years? There will be a cure for every disease. People will live longer, but they will eventually die of old age. There will be cars, trucks, boats, airplanes and trains for all the fleshly people who live here. Everybody will be at peace with one another; all the animals will be as tame as a pussycat. Even the lion and the bear can sleep with the lamb. A little girl can go to a big tiger and lead him around like a tame house cat, and if she gets tired she can lie on his belly and go to sleep.

All the animals' appetites will change. I imagine that they all will eat grass. They all will be tame, and they won't eat other animals or people.

Remember the story of King Nebuchadnezzar—when his mind was distorted (he was crazy), they tied him to a stump of a tree, and he ate grass.[13] If grass sustained him for seven years, I'm sure it will sustain all the animals.

This time will be like the Garden of Eden. I don't know if the snake will still be on its belly. When the snake was created, it had only a small portion of its tail on the ground. But after Satan used the snake to tempt Eve, God cursed the snake. He made it crawl on the ground and eat dust as well as put fear in the woman.[14]

The people of the earth will take all the tanks, guns and everything you can think of related to war machinery, and they will melt them down to make farm machinery. They will study war no more.[15]

I believe all the thistles and weeds will fall off the land. I think everybody will be able to farm organic; they could probably junk all their spray machinery.

---

13 Daniel 4:33.
14 Genesis 3:14–15.
15 Micah 4:3.

However, the influence Satan had on everybody will still have an impact on how they conduct themselves. Even though they don't have the devil to torment them, there still will be books, videos and dirty things left. That's why Christ Jesus will rule with a rod of iron. So the earth will go on as it does today. The sun will come up and go down. It will rain and snow, and the weather will be normal for the four seasons. I don't believe there will be floods, tornadoes, strong winds, volcanoes and earthquakes as happen today. Instead, this beautiful weather will go on for a thousand years!

I imagine that the earth will be heavily populated again during these thousand years.

Afterwards, Jesus will let the devil out of the bottomless pit for a short season, and he (the devil) will gather people from the four corners of the earth for a battle against Jesus and the saints. They will want to fight against Him. But Jesus will just speak, and Satan will be defeated. Then Jesus will throw the devil into the lake of fire where the Beast and the false prophet will be, and they shall be tormented for ever and ever for all eternity.[16]

Jesus will know who was for Him and who was against Him.

Also coming is the great white throne judgment of people from every tribe and race who rejected Jesus from the beginning of time to the end of the thousand years. This is when people will call for the rocks and hills and mountains to fall on them, to hide them from His face, the King of kings and Lord of lords.[17]

People will bow down and realize that He is God, but it will be too late. It will be to no avail because they rejected Him during their lifetime. Then God will throw them into eternal judgment for ever and ever. Yes, I'm saying that they will go to hell with everlasting fire!

---

16 Revelation 20:10.
17 Revelation 6.

Then God will bring the New Jerusalem down to earth, which is 1,500 miles high and 1,500 miles wide with twelve floors. We Christians will all go there; that will be the headquarters for all eternity. After that God will refurbish the earth. He will burn up everything in it with fervent heat, and then He will make it all new again like the Garden of Eden. I don't think the sun will shine, for God's presence will be on all the earth, and who knows what He has in store for all of us.[18]

I did talk to some theologians years ago, and the question was raised about the stars being populated. They said that they believe that would be possible. Remember when God told Abraham that his descendants would be as the sands of the sea?[19] I think I could hold all the Jews in a five-gallon bucket if each grain of sand represented a Jew at this present time. So how many people would it take to match the sands of the sea? I don't think God exaggerates, but that's my little theory.

---

18 Revelation 21 and 22.
19 Genesis 22:17.

The Bible says that we can't even think or conceive what is ahead.[20] We don't have the brain capacity to comprehend what He has for us. But even so, Lord Jesus, come quickly.

If you are here on this earth and all the little children and babies and Christians have disappeared, then you've got to believe what I said is true.

Tell Jesus that you are a sinner and ask Him to forgive you. Tell Him that you believe He died for you, that He rose from the dead, and that He is coming back again!

But please don't wait until all the Christians have left this world.

Do it now!

---

20 1 Corinthians 2:9.